Mommy Says...
I Can Be Anything

by Archita Allen Graves & Alysia Faith Allen

Illustrated by MikeMotz.com

We dedicate this book to the best mother and nana
that a girl could ask for, Yvonne McNeill Allen.
Thank you for loving us enough to say no
and supporting us when you say yes.
You're an amazing person.
We love you 7!
Love,
Your Big Baby & Nana's Girl

Mommy Says... I Can Be Anything

by Archita Allen Graves & Alysia Faith Allen

Illustrated by MikeMotz.com

Special thanks to our family and friends for their
support & encouragement. To James W. Graves,
husband & father, your love & support made
this book possible. We love you, Man of God.

Lastly, a special thank you to Peaches Dean.
Your kindness and friendship made our dream a reality.
Thank you for sharing your wisdom
and illustrator with us.

Heavenly Father, there are not enough words
to thank You for everything that You do,
but we'll start with this book.
~A.G. & A.A.

Thank you Nana & DaDa.
I love you to infinity & beyond!
~Alysia

EAN-13: 978-1500858452

Printed in the U.S.A.

My mommy says that I can be
anything that I want to be.
She says that I can do anything
and that the sky's the limit for me.

My mommy says that I can be a painter
if that's what I want to do.

So why is it that she yells "Stop!"
every time I try to?

My mommy says that I can be a chef
and cook dinner for the President.

So why is it that when I try to practice she yells
"Don't you touch that stove!" with her southern accent?

My mommy says that I can be a veterinarian
and help sick animals if I want.

So why is it that when I try to practice
on my dog she yells "No! Don't!"?

My mommy says that I can be a detective
if that's what I choose to do.

So why is it that she yells "Stop being nosey, Alysia!" every time I try to?

I'm starting to see a pattern here.
Maybe I'm too small.

Maybe I'll just try again in a few years
when I'm big and tall.

My mommy says that I can be anything,
and I believe that's true.

But before I take such a big step,
maybe I should first learn how to tie my shoe.

Draw and color Alysia.

What does your mommy say that you can be when you grow up? Draw a picture.

My Mommy says that I can be…

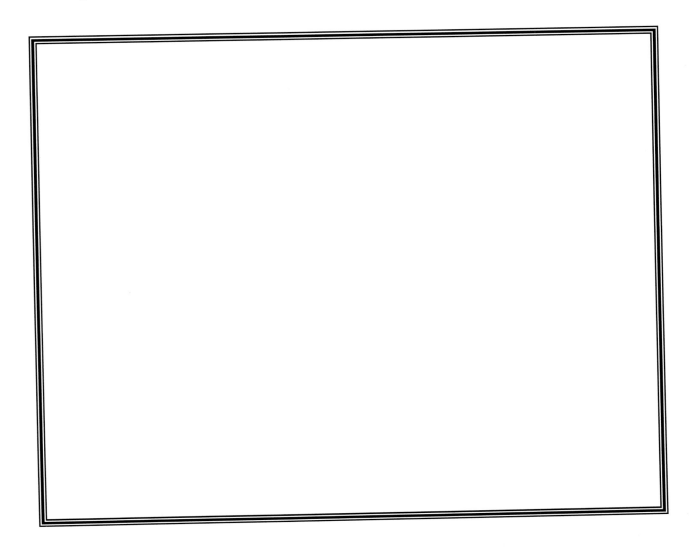

Draw a picture of you and your mommy.

What do you love about yourself? Draw a picture.

ABOUT THE AUTHORS

Archita L. Graves is an Army veteran and the founder/executive director of NATAI Girl, a mentorship program in Fayetteville, North Carolina. In addition to her philanthropic efforts in Fayetteville, she plans to expand NATAI Girl to her childhood hometown of Sanford, North Carolina in the fall of 2014. Archita truly believes that a woman who knows her worth is an unstoppable force which explains why she invests in the lives of young girls. She resides in Fayetteville with her husband, James Graves, and her daughter Alysia Faith. For more information, Archita can be contacted at agraves@nataigirl.org.

Alysia Faith Allen is a fourth grader at Harvest Preparatory Academy. In addition to writing stories, she also enjoys Bible stories and spending time with her Nana. Alysia Faith started collecting and distributing blankets to the homeless Christmas Eve of 2012 through her organization, Blankets of Faith. She resides in Fayetteville with her parents, James & Archita Graves.

Made in the USA
Columbia, SC
27 November 2018